Scrambled eggs?
NOOOOO!
NO!
WAYOOOH! WAY

OK, pour the powder in this valve.
This better work.
FIRE
I think it will.
Powder in system.
Hector, now!
Here we go!
FIRE
WAYO
WAYOOOH

AGHHHHH!!!

FWOMP!
Success!

Say goodbye!
AGHHHHH!!!
Don't worry, Dee, we'll save you!

HA! Gotcha!
Let me go!
C'mon, mathletes! Hurry up!

I have powdered eggs, but what do we do?
You keep powdered eggs on you?
You never know when you'll need 'em. Case in point!
I have an idea! Follow me!

I'll break your calculator in two!
OK, fine. They're allergic to eggs!

Thanks, Bubba!
BONK!

Give me the girl!
Stay where you are!

Mustard
Grappling
Hook
clink
POOF!

That trophy is OURS!
MATH BOWL
HELP!

MATH BOWL
Any idea how to take these things down?
I'm working on it!
DEE!
AGHHHH!!!
DEE!

Jelly Bean
Shrapnel

POW!
POW!
BLAM!
BLAM!

RRRRIIIP!
WOO-YAH!
MATH BOWL

POW!
HIIYAAAH!

BONK!
How do you stop the mutants?
I'm not sayin'!
Man, your breath smells like coffee!

CHOMP!

Not so fast, Bubba!
Pancake Disk

HIIYAAAH!
Tong Sais
BOOF!
BOOF!

WHOOSH!
PEAS

Smoke Can of Peas
CLINK-
CLINK-

Peas?
?
CLINK-

HHHHHHHHHHH!!!

AGHHHHHHH
That trophy is *ours*!
Dee, j-j-just give them the trophy!
No way! It's ours!

Nobody defeats Willowby Academy! NOBODY!

Looks like *these* public-school kids won!

You are correct! Thompson Brook takes the championship!
Here's the trophy!
MAT BOW
MATH BOWL
SNAP!
CLAP! CLAP! CLAP! CLAP!

If x plus twenty-one equals thirty-three . . .
. . . what does x equal?
TWELVE!

Two hundred fifty!
Correct! With one equation left, we have a tied game!
The final mathletes, please!

Twenty-two!
Correct! Point for Thompson Brook. Thompson Brook now trails by one point.
Next mathletes, please.
Fifty times five equals what?

Look at the size of the audience out there!
How are we going to keep our identities a secret?
I brought these masks!
Good thinking, Betty!
I'm climbing up to the stage lighting. You cover backstage.
Time to divide and conquer!

Betty, what's the score?
Lunch Lady! Am I relieved to see you! Willowby is ahead by a few points.
Correct! Point for Willowby.
Good gravy! I'm afraid of what will happen if Willowby loses.
There's no telling how Addison's mutant creations will react.

Half of eighty-two is what?
Forty-one!
Correct. Point for Willowby Academy.
Five hours past eight a.m. is what time?
Two p.m.!
I'm sorry, that is incorrect.
One p.m.!
Correct, Willowby!
Seven times seven is what?
Forty-nine!
Correct again, Willowby!
One-third of ninety-nine is what?
Thirty-three!
Another correct answer from Willowby!
Twenty times twenty is what?
Four hundred.
Willowby is unstoppable!

Five!
Correct. Point for Thompson Brook.
A dozen dogs have how many legs?
Forty-eight!
Corr
If Johnny had twenty apples and gave one to each of his eighteen classmates, how many apples would he have left?
Two!
Correct. Point for Willowby Academy.
The library checks out twenty books per day. How many books are checked out in two weeks?
Two hundred eighty!
Correct, Thompson Brook.

Thompson Brook! Orson, Jacob, Karen, Hector, Terrence, and Dee!
Not now, Betty!
Oh, cashew nuts!
Let's begin. What is one hundred divided by twenty?

Huddle up, Thompson Brook! I want you to know that I'm proud of you no matter what happens tonight. Go out there and give it your best!
And let's meet our teams! First, defending champions—Willowby Academy! Bill, Dena, Ella, Liam, Eduardo, and Stacy!
And the challengers . . .
Mr. O'Connell!
Go get 'em, guys!

Why don't you just forfeit, O'Connell?
I ♡ MATH
Thompson Brook Mathletes don't give up!
Guys, I found nothing!
And you looked through all their bags?
Even Addison's briefcase.
We're in for it.

"Where the city's brightest go head to head in a math frenzy!"
Pardon me.
Just trying to get to my seat.
Betty, come in, Betty.
"These students have fought hard all season long."
I'm here, Lunch Lady.
Mole Communicator
The Willowby Mathletes aren't human! They'll do *anything* to win! We need to stop the Math Bowl! This could get dangerous!
"And they're here tonight to win the title!"
I'll do my best!
I'm on my way!

MATH BOWL

Meanwhile, across town at the Civic Center . . .
Welcome to the annual Math Bowl!

Get outta heah, Lunch Lady!
Pay no mind. This is a janitor thing!
But–?!

KALOWSKI?!
THWOCK!
My mop!
SNAP!

Willowby Academy. Does. Not. LOSE!
Vladimir, let her go!

Floors may be slippery when wet!
SLOSH!
THUD!

Buster, you don't know who you're messing with!
Pineapple Mace

I need to get outta here and to the Math Bowl!
IIIYAAAH!
BONK!

Hey, lady, you're going to regret ever seeing Addison's lab! You know I can't let you leave now, right?
What does this all mean?

It means your mathletes are doomed! We here at Willowby Academy are winners!
OOOOF!

Sweet BBQ sauce!
What in the horseradish?! They're some kind of weird bio-pods. This can't be good for the Thompson Brook Mathletes.
LIFE-POD 3000
LIFE-POD 3000
LIFE-POD 3000
LIFE-POD 3000
LIFE-POD 3000

Mr. Addison's classroom
Let's see what I can find.
How odd. A switch under his desk? Wonder what it does.
A secret door behind the chalkboard?
RRRRRRRRRRRRRR

A trophy case!
Ice Cream Scoop Flashlight
Photos of Addison's winning mathletes.
Moldy bread!
Twenty years of mathletes and they all have the same weird green eye color.

That afternoon at Willowby Academy . . .
Another fine day of education! Bring us home another win, Mr. Addison!
Thank you, Headmaster Randall. See you over at the Math Bowl!
Coast is clear!
Cannoli-oculars

BRRRIIIIIIIIIIING!
Good luck tonight, math losers!
Hope your calculators don't break from all that math!
Good one, Milmoe!
Hope your face doesn't break from playing all that football that you play!
T, leave the witty comebacks to me.

Good afternoon, Thompson Brook students!

Tonight is the big Math Bowl! Surely it will all *add* up to *equal* a victory for our mathletes!
#1 Principal

Not a single trace of a single student after they left Willowby Academy? That's a little strange!
Well, computers can only get us so far. I'm headed to Willowby Academy to snoop around.
I'll meet you at the Math Bowl tonight, Betty.
You got it! I'll hang back here and clean the dishes!
CLICK

In the Boiler Room . . .
This is odd, Betty. I can't find records on any of Addison's former mathletes.
Watermelons!
You would think such bright students would go on to college or something.
Addison's teams have bee
winning since he started
teaching twenty-somethin
years ago.

I just hope the kids aren't disappointed.
TEACHERS' LOUNGE
We need to win this for Mr. O'Connell!
Definitely!
Addison seems like an ordinary math teacher— his breath smells like coffee, his nose hairs are long . . .
But something's up! It's strange that they've never lost a match.
Let's keep our eyes open tonight.

The next day in the teachers' lounge . . .
I don't know how we're going to do it.
Willowby hasn't lost a championship—not once!
Our mathletes are good, but Mr. Addison is ruthless.

Six!
Correct!
Twenty-seven!
Correct!
Two hundred!
Correct!
Finally, for the win . . .
Three divided by two is what?
1.5!
Correct!
Yay, Dee!
Don't touch me, Orson!
Thompson Brook wins and advances to the Math Bowl Championship!

That night . . .
Welcome to the semifinals. It's Thompson Brook versus Heard Street School.
Go, Thompson Brook!
Let's begin! Twelve times ten equals what?
120!
Correct!
How many doughnuts are in two dozen?
Twenty-four!
Correct!

Gravy?
On fish sticks?!

Gravy?
That's my boy!
You know it, Betty!
Hector, you are sick!

At lunch . . .
Extra fish sticks for the mathletes!
Thanks, Lunch Lady!
You'll need the brainpower for tonight's Math Match!
It's the semifinals! The winner goes on to the Math Bowl!

If a train has 120 miles to travel, how many miles until the train is halfway to its destination?
Sixty!
Correct! Thompson Brook wins!
In soccer, eleven players are allowed on the field from each team. What would be the maximum number of players on the field?
Twenty-two!
Correct! Another win for Thompson Brook!

Over the following weeks, the Thompson Brook Mathletes are on a roll!
Twenty ducks are in a pond. Five fly away. How many ducks are left?
Fifteen!
Correct!
For the win, five plus two plus four equals what?
Eleven!
Correct! Another win for Thompson Brook!

Looks like there's some history between those two.
Pffft! Public-school kids.
I think we'll make that *team* history. It's on!

Hello, Mr. Addison.
How's everything at Willowby Academy?
Good.
How's that trophy case over at Thompson Brook?
Still empty?
HAHAHAHA HAHAHAHAHA!
I ♥ MATH

As you know, the Willowby Academy Mathletes are unstoppable. We've got a match later this afternoon.
I ♡ MATH

You did it, guys! Our first victory!
Yeah!
Happy dance!
Good work, Dee.
Whatever. Let's get out of here
Don't get used to it, O'Connell.

If a pet store sold ten goldfish a day for a week, how many goldfish would they sell?
You can do it, Dee!
Sixty!
I'm sorry, Jackson Street School answered incorrectly. For the win, Thompson Brook, do you have an answer?
Pfft.
It's seventy.
Not like I care.
Thompson Brook wins!
Woo.
YES!
WOOT! WOOT!
Yay!

That night at the Math Match . . .
If a pizza had ten slices and I ate four of them, how many slices of pizza would be left?
Six!
Excellent! Another point for Thompson Brook!
YES!
Next mathletes, please.
Good job, Hector!

Off to class, kids. I'll grab your trays!
Lunch Lady . . .
Thanks, Lunch Lady!
. . . What can I do to psych up the kids?
They'll come around.
Hmph!!
Well, good morning, Mr. Kalowski.
Comin' through!
I have to get to class. Thanks again for the cookies!

Hey! There are my rookie mathletes!
Eat up! Big night tonight!
Our first Math Match!
I'll be there. Go, team!
BRRRIIIIIIINNG

Like it or not, math is everywhere you go.
That's true! I needed to know how many cups of water to add to the powder to make these scrambled eggs this morning.
Mmmm.
Yum.
PLOP,

The next day at breakfast . . .
Good morning, Breakfast Bunch! How did it go yesterday?
The cookies were good.
It was painful!
The punishment does not fit the crime!

Quick! What does five times fifty equal?
250!
Good! We'll need to think fast if we expect to get to the quarterfinals this year.
Dee-quick! What does ten times ten equal?
Um . . . a pencil stabbing my eye?
Ooooh! Ooooh! I know this one!
Dee, I know you know this. We'll need to work as a team if we want to win.
It's easy! One hundred!

Wow! Thanks, Lunch Lady!
Lunch Lady, these are delicious!
Hmph!
Well, good luck, mathletes!
OK, kids, time to let our math flags fly high!

I understand you know Orson.
That's Jacob
and Karen.
Hi, Dee.
Super.
Let's get our math on!
Tewiffic!
MR. O'CONNELL
Thought all this math might make everyone hungry! Maybe we can add some cookies to the mix?

Hector! Terrence! Dee! So glad to have you as mathletes!
Welcome!
Meet the team!

I'd almost say that hurt my feelings.
If I cared what Milmoe thought.
Milmoe thinks?
C'mon, guys, let's get this over with.
Here we are.
On the count of three . . . Oh. Sorry. That's more math.
MR. O'CONNELL

After school . . .
Are you guys ready for this?
Is ten the square root of one hundred?
HECTOR!
Too soon?
Hey, McKenna, look! It's the mathlympians, or whatever they call themselves. Math-LAME-ians! HA! HA!
Let's get to football practice!
Good one, Milmoe!
15

Those kids ditched out on the tour on their own.
That's true. But they always seem to be getting us out of jams. Fire up the mixer, Betty. We can at least bake them some cookies.
Aye, aye, Captain!

Who would voluntarily choose to do math after school?
You'd have to be insane!
This is way worse than detention!
MILK-CAM
Way worse!
I feel terrible, Betty!
Worse than a soggy French fry!
It's not your fault, Lunch Lady.

Eavesdropping? No! I volunteer to help sharpen Secretary Louanne's pencils.
Thanks, sweetie!
See you guys at Mathletes!
PERSEVERANCE

WHOA!

Orson, were you eavesdropping?
Oh . . . uh, hi, Dee!

Your parents agree that this is a generous decision.
The first mathletes practice will be after school today in Mr. O'Connell's classroom.
Now please return to class.
Yes, sir, Principal Hernandez.

I was terribly disappointed to learn that you three skipped out on the museum tour. I have reviewed my options and have come up with a disciplinary action.
#1 Principal

You are to join the mathletes team.

LADY

and the Mutant Mathletes

Jarrett J. Krosoczka

Alfred A. Knopf New York

LUNCH
POW!

Meanwhile . . .
Sure is a nice day for an ice cream, Betty.
Bakery
OPEN
JIMMY'S
OPEN
Sure is!
JIMMY'S
?
!
Uh-oh!

Everybody freeze! Give us all of the money outta the register!
No funny business, just put the cash in the bags!
Y-y-yes, s-s-sir.
I'll take some of this ice cream while you're at it!

Daddy, could I please have an ice cream, pleeeease?!
OK, I don't see why not.
OPEN

One swirl soft-serve on a cone, please.
Yes, sir!
CLOSED